THE WIND
IN THE
WILLOWS

Retold by Barbara Hayes

Brown Watson

ENGLAND

Mr Toad's New Caravan

One morning, the Mole who had been working hard, spring-cleaning his little underground home, suddenly cried out "Bother!" and "O blow" and "Hang spring-cleaning!" Then, he bolted out of the house without putting on his coat and ran away from his dear home, looking for something more interesting to do than housework. Luckily, along the way he met the Water Rat who lived in a cosy hole at the edge of a river.

The Water Rat was a dear fellow. He invited the Mole to stay with him. They had great times together. Sometimes they went fishing and sometimes they visited the Rat's friends, one of whom was Mr Toad.

Mr Toad was a dear fellow, too. He was rich and generous and lived in a grand house, but he was not very sensible. He was always having crazes for things and he would keep on boasting so! The Mole and the Rat often sat chuckling about the foolish things Toad did. But they could not help liking him in spite of his boastful ways.

One morning, the Rat and the Mole decided to row up the river to visit Mr Toad at Toad Hall. "It's never the wrong time to call on Toad. Early or late, he's always glad to see you," said the Rat, "and he's always sorry when you go." They rowed past the water-mill and walked across the lawns to Toad Hall. "Hooray!" cried Toad on seeing them. "How lucky that you arrived now. I have discovered the thing I want to spend the rest of my life with." He had only just got up and was still wearing his dressing gown. He led the friends into the stable yard where a gypsy caravan stood glittering in the sunshine.

"There!" beamed Toad. "I want to spend the rest of my life travelling in this little cart. I shall roll along the open road, between the hedgerows, to villages, towns and cities. Here today and somewhere else tomorrow!" The Mole was tremendously excited and thought Toad's idea was wonderful. "I have packed everything we need and we can start this afternoon," said Toad. "What do you mean 'we' and 'start this afternoon'?" said the Rat. "I have no plans to go on a caravan trip."

"Now dear, good old Ratty," said Toad, "don't talk in that sniffy way. You know you've got to come. I can't possibly manage without you." And, after much chatting, Mole and Rat agreed to go with Mr Toad.

It was a golden afternoon. Birds called to them from the orchards on either side of the road. Rabbits sitting at their front doors in the hedgerows held up their forepaws and sighed, "O my! O my!"

Everything went well all that day, that night and the next morning, except that Mr Toad left all the work to the Rat and the Mole. The Rat missed his dear home at the riverside but he didn't complain. "We will stick by Toad until he is tired of the caravan," whispered the Rat to Mole. "It will soon be over. His fads never last long."

The end was even nearer than expected. That very afternoon, as they were rolling along the highway, they heard from behind, a faint, warning hum, like the drone of a bee. Glancing back, they saw a cloud of dust advancing on them at great speed, while from out of the dust came a faint 'Poop-poop!' In what seemed like an instant, the cloud of dust caught up with them in a huge gust of wind and a 'poop-poop' rang with a brazen shout in their ears.

Startled out of their wits, they jumped into the nearest ditch and just had time to glimpse a magnificent motor-car hurtle past and then dwindle to a speck in the distance where they heard the roar turn back into a droning hum. The horse pulling the caravan reared in alarm. The caravan overturned and was wrecked and the Rat was furious.

He was telling Mr Toad that he should make the car owners pay for every penny of damage when the Rat and the Mole saw that Mr Toad was in a dream. He was sitting in the middle of the dusty road, staring after the motor-car and murmuring 'Poop-poop! Poop-poop!' Mr Toad did not care at all about his wrecked caravan. He had a new craze - motor-cars! "Motor-cars are the only way to travel," he murmured. "Here today, and in next week tomorrow!" Then, leading the horse, they set off for home.

Badger to the Rescue

The Rat and the Mole took Mr Toad safely back to Toad Hall and then went back to Rat's home by the river-bank. They took things easy for a while, doing a little boating and a little fishing, until the Rat spoke with an old friend. At once he hurried home to the Mole. "I have news," he said. "There's nothing else being talked about all along the river-bank. Toad has bought a very expensive motor-car!"

Unfortunately, Mr Toad did not have the patience to learn to drive properly. He crashed one beautiful car after another. His stables became full of old wrecks. His friends were worried about him. Not only was he wasting his money, he was risking his life and the lives of others. Word of Mr Toad's dangerous and foolish ways even reached along the dark pathways into the Wild Wood where Mr Badger lived. Mr Badger was important and sometimes rather frightening.

One bright morning in the early part of summer, a heavy knock sounded at the door of the Water Rat's home. The Mole went to open it and the Rat heard him give a cry of surprise, before he stepped back into the parlour and announced with much importance: "Mr Badger!"

The Rat sat open-mouthed. Mr Badger hardly ever came visiting.

"The hour has come," announced Mr Badger in a serious voice. "What hour?" asked the Rat, glancing uneasily at the clock on the mantlepiece. "Toad's hour, of course," replied the Badger. "The hour to take Toad in hand and make him stop all this foolishness with cars. I've just heard he's crashed yet another car. You two must come with me at once to Toad Hall and the work of rescuing Toad must begin."

"Right you are!" cried the Rat, jumping up. He and the Mole tidied and locked up home and set out with Mr Badger.

They reached the drive of Toad Hall to find a brand new shiny motor-car of great size standing in front of the house. Mr Toad, dressed in the newest and flashiest of motoring clothes, came swaggering down the steps. "Hello, you fellows," he cried cheerfully, as he saw the Rat, the Mole, and the Badger. "You are just in time to come for a jolly ride in my new car."

"Take him inside," Badger said to the Rat and the Mole, and as the amazed Toad was dragged up the steps, Badger spoke to the driver of the car.

"You won't be wanted today," he said. "Mr Toad has changed his mind. He will not require this car. Please take it away." Then Badger followed the others inside and shut the door. He told Toad to take off his motoring clothes.

"Shan't," replied Toad.

"Take them off him, you two." Badger said to the Rat and the Mole. It was no easy task. They had to put Toad on the floor and drag the motoring clothes off him item by item. They sat him in a chair and the Badger spoke to him firmly. "You knew it would come to this sooner or later, Toad," said Badger. "You have taken no notice of the warnings I have sent to you. You have gone on wasting the money your father left to you. You are getting the area a bad name with all your fast driving and smashes and quarrels with the police. Now I want you to say in front of us, your friends, that you are sorry for your behaviour and you now see that it was stupid."

There was a long pause while Toad looked desperately this way and that for a way out, but there was none. Still he would not give in. "No!" he said, "I'm not sorry. It wasn't stupid. It was glorious."

"Very well, then," said Badger, "if talking to you is no good, we will use force. We will lock you in your bedroom and we will stay and look after you, until you are over this motor-car craze and are your old self again."

11

Badger, Rat and Mole took it in turns to sleep in Toad's bedroom every night and divided up between them the task of watching him by day. At first Toad was very trying to his dear friends. When the desire to drive a car had hold of him, he would arrange the bedroom chairs into the shape of a car. Then he would crouch on them making car noises and screaming 'Poop-poop.' Finally he would turn a somersault and lie still amongst the upset chairs.

As time passed, however, these wild games stopped. His friends tried chatting with him about other things like boating and picnics on the river and games of cricket. Toad was not interested. He stopped being interested in anything. He took to staying in bed, looking pale and ill, and saying he wanted to be left alone. One day, Rat went upstairs to take over the watching from Badger, so that Badger and Mole could go out for some fresh air. Toad was still in bed and saying he felt ill, but that no one was to worry about him.

"You look out, Rat," said Badger. "When Toad is quiet he is at his most artful. He's sure to try one of his tricks. Be careful. Oh well now, we must be off." Badger and Mole went out leaving Rat on guard, and the Rat went to speak to the pale Mr Toad.

"How are you today, old chap?" he asked.

"Oh, how I am doesn't matter. How are you, and dear Mole?" came the reply.

Rat said that the Mole was fine and that he was out with Badger. Mr Toad knew then that he and the Rat were alone in the house. This was his chance. He pretended that he was so ill he needed a doctor. The worried Rat hurried out of the bedroom, but was careful to lock the door behind him, just to be on the safe side. Really, he thought, Toad was far too ill to try to escape.

But Toad was not ill. He watched the Rat leave, then got dressed, filled his pockets with money from the dressing table drawer, made a rope of knotted sheets and climbed down from the window.

Toad steals a Car

Toad hurried away from
Toad Hall as fast as he could.
After several miles, he came
to the Red Lion Inn and
went in for a meal. As he
was finishing he heard the
poop-poop of a car as it
turned into the inn-yard. The
driver and his passenger got
out to stretch their legs and
chat about how wonderful
driving was.

Toad listened eagerly and
at last he could stand it no longer. He paid for his meal and slipped out
to look at the motor-car. "There cannot be any harm in just looking at
it," he thought. The car stood in the middle of the yard quite alone. By
then its owner had gone into the inn for some food. As if in a dream,
Toad found himself starting the car engine and driving off.

He felt wonderful. He was really free again. He did not care that he was doing wrong. He only knew that he was the mighty Toad once more, Toad the terror, Toad at his best, before whom all must give way. He drove faster and faster, not caring where he went as long as he was driving a car.

But of course, it all ended in

tears. Toad was caught. Toad was seized by the police. The car was taken from him and returned to its owners.

Then Toad was put on trial before the magistrates in a far-off town where no one knew him. He was found guilty of stealing a car, driving to the public danger, and of being cheeky to the police. He was sent to prison for twenty years, which is a very long time.

Toad was put in chains, taken to a grim old castle and pushed down some stone steps into a cold, dark dungeon. He was filled with despair. He wept bitter tears. How he wished he had listened to Badger and Rat and Mole.

For several weeks, Toad refused any meals, although the old jailer, who knew that Toad had plenty of money on him, offered to have any comfort or tasty luxury brought in which Toad might fancy. He said anything nice could be arranged at a price.

But Toad was not interested. All he wanted was to be free, free to drive big fast cars along the open road. At last the jailer grew tired of trying to please Toad. He grumbled to his daughter, who, as it happened, often helped her father with little jobs about the prison and was also very fond of animals.

"Father, I can't bear to see that poor toad so unhappy and so thin. You let me have the managing of him. I'll make him eat from my hand," she said. Her father replied that she could do as she liked.

That very day the jailer's daughter knocked at the door of Toad's cell. "Now cheer up, Toad, and be a sensible animal," she said. "I've brought you some bubble and squeak hot from the stove." The smell of the food was wonderful, but still Toad would not eat. The jailer's daughter took the food away again, but the smell lingered in Toad's cell, reminding him of how good life could be. When the girl came back with tea and buttered toast, Toad gobbled it up.

He ate well for several days. He told the jailer's daughter about Toad Hall and how rich and clever he was. The kind girl listened to all his boasting, then told him she had an aunt who was a washerwoman. "She does the washing for the prison and if you are as rich as you say, you could slip her a few pounds. It would be nothing to you, but would mean a lot to her. Next time she comes here, she could give you some of her clothes and you could escape by pretending to be the prison washerwoman. You are quite like my aunt, especially about the figure."

"I'm not," said Toad in a huff. "I have an elegant figure, for what I am."

"So has my aunt for what she is," replied the girl "and you should not be so proud and horrid when I am trying to help you." Toad had to agree that she was right.

The next evening the aunt came to Toad's cell. Toad gave her money and she gave him clothes. Then the washerwoman said they should tie her up so it would seem she had given the clothes unwillingly from the weekly wash. Toad dressed up in the dress and apron and shawl and black bonnet.

The jailer's daughter gave him a bagful of washing and her aunt's umbrella. She told him to go out the way she had come in and wished him goodbye and good luck. With a quaking heart and as firm a footstep as he could manage, Toad walked up the stone steps and past the guards. He was free.

Toad immediately thought how clever he was to have escaped, quite forgetting the plan had been the jailer's daughter's. He made up a song which he sang as he hurried through woods and over fields.

A Car-Crash

"The world has had great heroes,
As history books have showed;
But never a name to go
down in fame
Compared with that of Toad!

The clever men at Oxford
Know all that there is to
be knowed.
But they none of them know
one half as much
As intelligent Mr Toad!"

There was a lot more, but it was all so boastful it is better not written down.

After some miles of country lanes, he reached the high road and as he turned into it and glanced along its length, he saw approaching him a speck that turned into a dot and then into a blob and then into something very familiar. It was a motor-car!

"This is more like it," Toad beamed, "I will wave them down and tell them some hard luck story and they will certainly not refuse to give an old lady a lift. Perhaps I may even end up being driven to Toad Hall in a motor-car! That will be one in the eye for Badger, and the Rat, and the Mole!" Slowly, the car came closer, and closer, and closer. Toad suddenly fell in a shaking heap of fear on the road.

The car was the very car he had stolen from outside the Red Lion Inn, and the people in it were the very same people. Luckily they did not recognise Toad in his washerwoman's clothes. They thought he was a poor old woman who had fainted, and they picked him up and gave him a lift. But, silly vain Toad could not be satisfied with his good luck. He made up his mind that he was going to drive that wonderful car again.

After a while he said: "I was wondering, if I might sit on the front seat beside the driver. There I could get the fresh air full in my face, and I should feel better much quicker."

"What a sensible woman," said the car owners. "Of course you shall sit in the front."

No sooner was Toad in the front of the car than he said to the driver: "Please, sir, I wish you would kindly let me drive this car for a little. I have been watching you carefully and it looks so easy. And I should like to be able to tell my friends that once I drove a very expensive motor-car!"

The driver and the others laughed, but then decided it would not hurt to let the old lady have a try at driving. How wrong they were! At first Toad drove slowly, but then he went a little faster and then a little faster still.

"Be careful, washerwoman!" called out the men. This annoyed Toad and he began to lose his head. He drove even faster and laughed and shouted in a loud voice.

"Washerwoman indeed! Ho, ho! I am Toad the motor-car snatcher, the prison-breaker, the entirely fearless Toad. Sit still and I will show you what driving really is!" With a cry of horror the men rose to their feet and flung themselves on Toad. Alas! They should have known better than to do that while the car was still speeding along the road. With a half-turn of the wheel Toad sent the car crashing into the thick mud of a horse pond. Toad was sent flying through the air to land on the soft, rich grass of a meadow. The men were left struggling in the muddy water held down by their long coats. By the time they were free, Toad had run far away across the fields, singing happily.

Toad immediately began to think how clever he was. "Ho, ho!" he laughed. "Toad has been wonderful again. Toad as usual has come out on top. Who managed to get a lift? Who managed to get on the front seat? Who persuaded them to let him drive the car? Why, Toad, of course. Clever Toad!" Then a slight noise made him turn his head. The car driver and two policemen were running after him.

The Rat saves Toad

Poor Toad ran on again, his heart in his mouth. He glanced back and saw to his dismay that the driver and policemen were gaining on him. He ran on desperately, but he was a fat animal and his legs were short. He could hear the men close behind him. Not even looking where he was going, he struggled on, glancing back over his shoulder every few seconds. Suddenly, the earth went from under his feet. He grasped at the air in vain. Splash! He found himself head over ears in deep water, rapid water, water that bore him along fast. Toad had run straight into the river. He tried to grasp the

rushes that grew along the water's edge, but the stream was so strong it tore them out of his hands. Presently he saw that he was approaching a big dark hole in the bank, just above his head. He reached up and caught hold of the edge. As he sighed and spluttered, a face with twinkling eyes came up from the hole. A hand grasped him and pulled him to safety. It was Water Rat.

As soon as he was standing safe and sound in the Water Rat's hallway, Toad started boasting about his adventures and how he had outwitted everyone he had met. The Rat just told him to go upstairs, clean himself and dress in some decent clothes from the Rat's cupboard.

By the time Toad came down again, lunch was on the table and very glad Toad was to see it, for it was a long time since he had eaten. While they ate, Toad told Rat all that had happened to him. The more he talked and boasted, the more grave and quiet the Rat became. When at last Toad had talked himself to a standstill, there was silence. Then the Rat said: "Now, Toady, I don't want to upset you after all you've been through, but seriously, don't you see what an awful ass you've been making of yourself? You know that you've never had anything but trouble from motor cars from the first moment you set eyes on one. When are you going to be sensible and think of your friends and try and be a credit to them?" Toad heaved a deep sigh.

"Quite right, Ratty," he said. "You are always so sound!"

"In any case," went on Toad, "I'm not so keen on motor-cars since I drove into that pond. Actually I've had a rather brilliant idea connected with motor-boats, but that can wait." The exhausted Toad went up to sleep in the spare bed and dreamed of his home, Toad Hall. Next day, while the Mole was finishing breakfast, Toad said that he thought he was strong enough to take a stroll home.

Rat and Mole looked at him in dismay, but before they could reply there was a knock at the door. It was Badger.

"Toad is back," said the Rat, "and he knows nothing about what has been happening at Toad Hall." Badger came in and told poor Toad that after word had got back that he had been put in prison, his home had been taken over by wicked Stoats and Weasels from the Wild Wood. Mole had bravely tried to turn them out, but it had been no good.

"You see, people took different sides when they knew you were in trouble," explained Badger. "The River-bankers, I mean the folks round here, friends of Ratty and Mole, stuck up for you, but the Wild Wood animals said hard things and said having your house taken over served you right for breaking the law. As we did not know when you were coming back, it was difficult to know what to do." Toad flung himself on the sofa in floods of tears. The Rat and Mole and Badger looked at each other seriously. Something had to be done.

"Fortunately," went on Badger, "'I used to go to Toad Hall in the old days, when Toad's father was alive. He showed me a secret passage which led in from the gardens to the kitchen. He said he had not told young Toad about it because he never could keep a secret." Toad hung his head. "Now that Toad is back," continued Badger, "I suggest that we arm ourselves with big sticks, creep into Toad Hall through the secret passage. Take the Wild Wood animals by surprise as they are at dinner and beat them with our sticks so much that they will never want to see Toad Hall again."

So that is what those good friends of Toad did. Toad Hall was cleared and made beautiful again. Toad went back to live there and promised to be good in future. He chose a handsome gold chain and locket set with pearls and sent it to the jailer's daughter to thank her for helping him. Badger went back to his home because he liked to be alone most of the time. And the Water Rat and the Mole went back to their happy life on the river.

Copyright © 1994 Martspress Ltd.
First published by Brown Watson, 1994
76 Fleckney Road, Kibworth Beauchamp, Leics, England.
Printed in Germany
ISBN 0-7097-0939-0